Disney

THE LITTLE MERMAID

Adventures ON LAND

By BRITTANY MAZIQUE

Screenplay by DAVID MAGEE

Based on Disney's *THE LITTLE MERMAID*

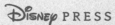 PRESS

LOS ANGELES • NEW YORK

All rights reserved. Published by Disney Press, an imprint of Buena Vista Books, Inc.
No part of this book may be reproduced or transmitted in any form or by any means,
electronic or mechanical, including photocopying, recording, or by any information
storage and retrieval system, without written permission from the publisher.
For information address Disney Press,
1200 Grand Central Avenue, Glendale, California 91201.

Printed in the United States of America

First Paperback Edition, April 2023

1 3 5 7 9 10 8 6 4 2

Library of Congress Control Number: 2022941048

ISBN 978-1-368-07725-5

FAC-029261-23055

For more Disney Press fun, visit www.disneybooks.com

One night when the sky was painted red by the Coral Moon, a mermaid named Ariel rescued a prince whose thirst for the sea matched her curiosity about life on land. Meeting Prince Eric intensified Ariel's desire to experience a world other than her own. So Ariel agreed to fall under the spell of the villainous sea witch, Ursula, and traded her voice for a chance to become human. But Ariel would have to kiss the prince within three days, or else she would belong to Ursula forever.

Ariel found herself tangled in a fisherman's net with Sebastian, her father's aide, at her side.

The fisherman looked at Ariel, who was covered in seaweed. "You poor thing. Must have washed ashore from the shipwreck," he said. "I'll take you to the castle. They'll know what to do with you."

Ariel opened her mouth to speak, but nothing came out. The fisherman wrapped her in a piece of sailcloth and, upon noticing Sebastian, casually tossed the crab into a crate. Ariel took one last look at the sea before she and Sebastian were carted off to the castle.

In the castle, Ariel marveled at things she was experiencing for the first time, like the warm glow of a fire. The castle's housekeepers, Lashana and Rosa, helped Ariel clean up and began to dress her in fresh clothes.

"Prince Eric is still looking for that girl who saved him," said Rosa. "Says he won't rest until he finds her."

Ariel listened with delight as Rosa pulled a dress over her head.

Lashana and Rosa looked at each other. Could this be the girl who had saved Eric? Lashana ran out of the room. She had to find the prince!

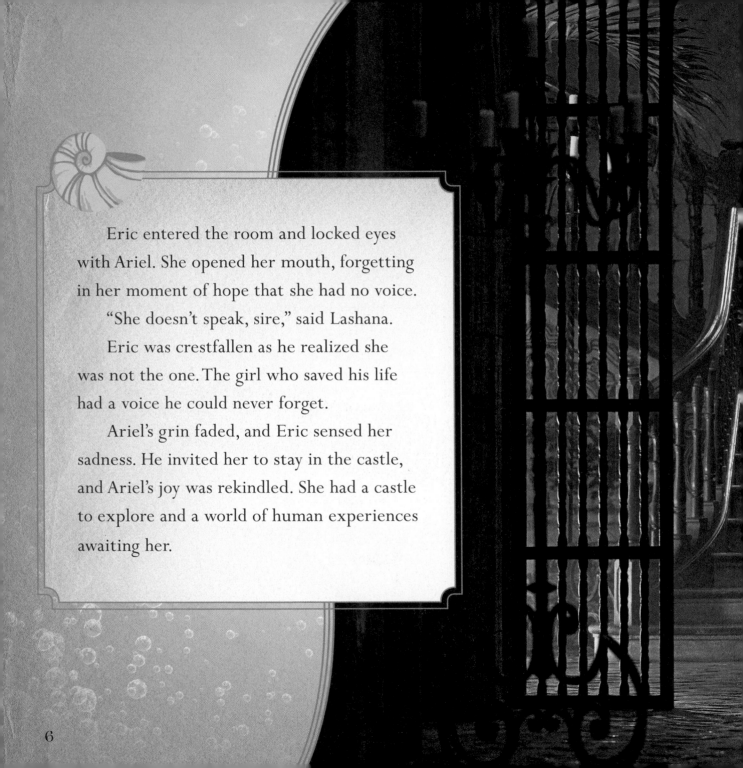

Eric entered the room and locked eyes with Ariel. She opened her mouth, forgetting in her moment of hope that she had no voice.

"She doesn't speak, sire," said Lashana.

Eric was crestfallen as he realized she was not the one. The girl who saved his life had a voice he could never forget.

Ariel's grin faded, and Eric sensed her sadness. He invited her to stay in the castle, and Ariel's joy was rekindled. She had a castle to explore and a world of human experiences awaiting her.

Later that day, a curious Ariel tiptoed down the castle's grand hallway and into a room filled with Eric's breathtaking objects. She was reminded of her own assortment of sunken items in her sea grotto.

She was mesmerized by the telescopes, globes, and figurines from faraway places—especially a miniature jade mermaid. Ariel delicately held the figurine in her hands as Sebastian skittered into the room. But before he could scold her for wandering around the castle, the door of the library swung open.

Sebastian and Ariel quickly hid.

"Who's in here?" It was Prince Eric.

Ariel stepped out of the shadow of the drapes.

Eric's eyes settled on Ariel holding the jade treasure. "My little mermaid," said Eric.

Ariel gasped before realizing Eric was speaking of the figurine.

"Isn't she beautiful?" he asked.

Eric pressed the little mermaid into her hand. "I'd like you to have her." He looked around the library at the items from his many voyages. "I know it must seem silly collecting all this stuff."

But Ariel did not think it was silly at all.

The orange and gold rays of the setting sun shone through the windows as Eric and Ariel grew closer to each other. He showed her sea stones made of shining amber, and they examined collections of shells from islands near and far.

Eric was impressed when Ariel created a long loud note by blowing in a conch, and she watched as he pointed on a map to uncharted lands he hoped to visit. While Eric wished to be at sea, Ariel wanted a life on land. Both of them longed to experience something new.

Eric pointed on the map to the main village and a beautiful lagoon with a waterfall. "I could show you around if you'd like. We'll go tomorrow."

Ariel couldn't hide the excitement in her eyes. Her dreams were within reach!

The next day, Sebastian was determined to break Ursula's spell. It could end with just one kiss. He secretly leaped into the carriage that carried Eric and Ariel down the village road. As Eric drove, Ariel watched in amazement. He offered Ariel the reins, and before he realized it, an exhilarated Ariel had taken control of the carriage.

Off they went at an alarming pace!

"Look out!" Eric shouted to an islander leading a donkey cart that Ariel narrowly missed.

She turned sharply, avoiding a roadside fruit stand but sending the carriage along the cliff's edge and nearly launching them through the air. Eric was impressed when Ariel brought the carriage to a sudden halt before they hit a herd of goats that blocked the road.

At the village market, Ariel was intrigued by the fragrant foods, vibrant fabrics, and energy of the crowd. A local band played music. Eric took Ariel's hand, and they danced to the rhythm of the steel drums.

Sebastian was certain that the two would kiss, but the moment passed. Ursula's spell was still not broken.

At the end of the night, Ariel and Eric made their way toward the staircase in the grand hallway of the castle, both still giddy from the adventures of the day. Before parting ways, they exchanged warm smiles.

Somewhere between the land and sea, a prince and a mermaid had been brought together to someday embark across uncharted waters. There was much to explore beyond the lives they were told they should live, and they were starting to hope that they could experience those adventures together.